# Using a Microscope

Heather Hammonds

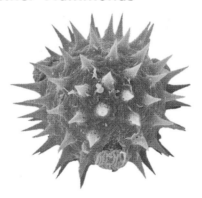

**NELSON**

TM

**THOMSON LEARNING**

Here is a microscope.

A microscope helps us

to see little things

that we can't see

with our eyes.

Here is a pond.

We can't see any bugs in it,

but they are there.

Using a microscope,

we can see the little bugs

that live in pond water.

Here is a little ant.

It is so small

that it is hard to see.

Using a microscope,

we can see

the little ant's body parts.

Here is some snow.

Snow is made up
of tiny snowflakes.

8

Using a microscope,

we can see

that every snowflake is different.

Here is a flower.

The pollen from the flower

can make us sneeze.

Using a microscope,

we can see

the little pollen grains.

Here is some sand.

Sand is made

of many small grains.

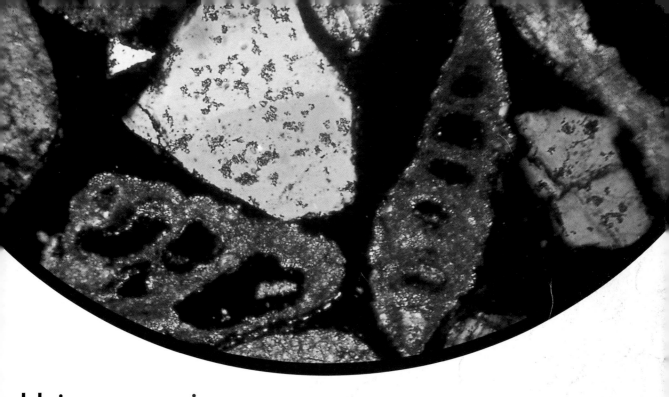

Using a microscope,

we can see

the little grains of sand.

Here is some old bread.

The bread is mouldy.

14

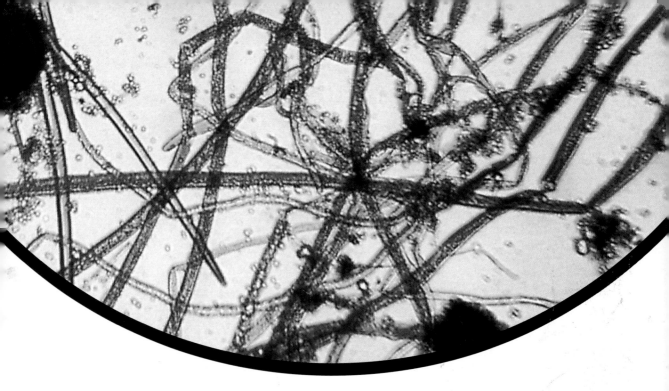

Using a microscope,

we can see

the little threads of mould.

15

A microscope makes very little things look big, and helps us to learn about them. What else can we look at?

**A leaf**

**A feather**